W9-BYM-394

DK

A DORLING KINDERSLEY BOOK

Written by Angela Royston
Photography by Steve Shott
Additional photography by Dave King
(pages 4-7 and 14-15)
Illustrations by Jane Cradock-Watson and Dave Hopkins

Aladdin Books
Macmillan Publishing Company
866 Third Avenue
New York, NY 10022

Macmillan Publishing Company is part of the
Maxwell Communication Group of Companies.

Eye Openers ™

First published in Great Britain in 1992
by Dorling Kindersley Limited,
9 Henrietta Street, London WC2E 8PS

Reproduced by Colourscan, Singapore
Printed and bound in Italy by L.E.G.O., Vicenza

1 2 3 4 5 6 7 8 9 10

ISBN 0-689-71565-X

Library of Congress
Catalog Card Number: 91-27724

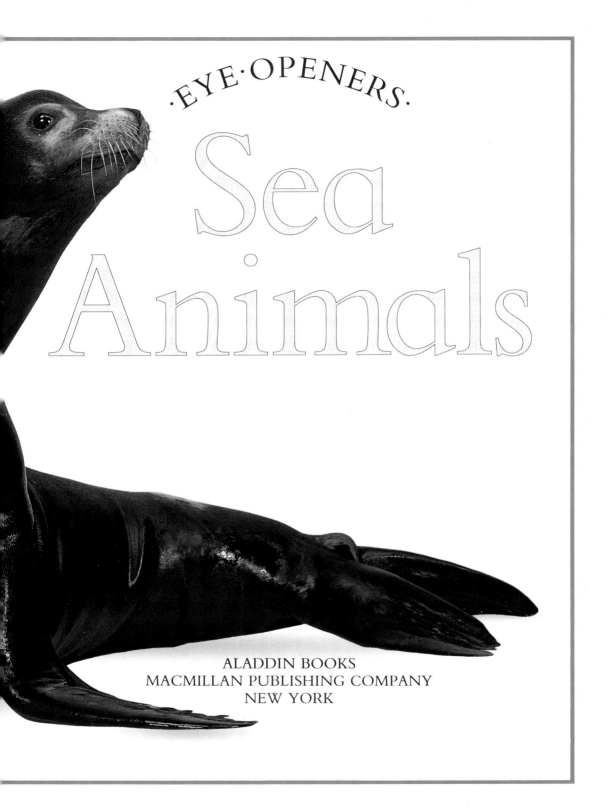

·EYE·OPENERS·

Sea Animals

ALADDIN BOOKS
MACMILLAN PUBLISHING COMPANY
NEW YORK

Dolphin

Dolphins are small whales.
They can swim very long
and fast without getting
tired. Dolphins are
intelligent and playful.
Large groups often leap
and dive next to ships.
Dolphins breathe through
the blowhole on top
of their heads.

flipper

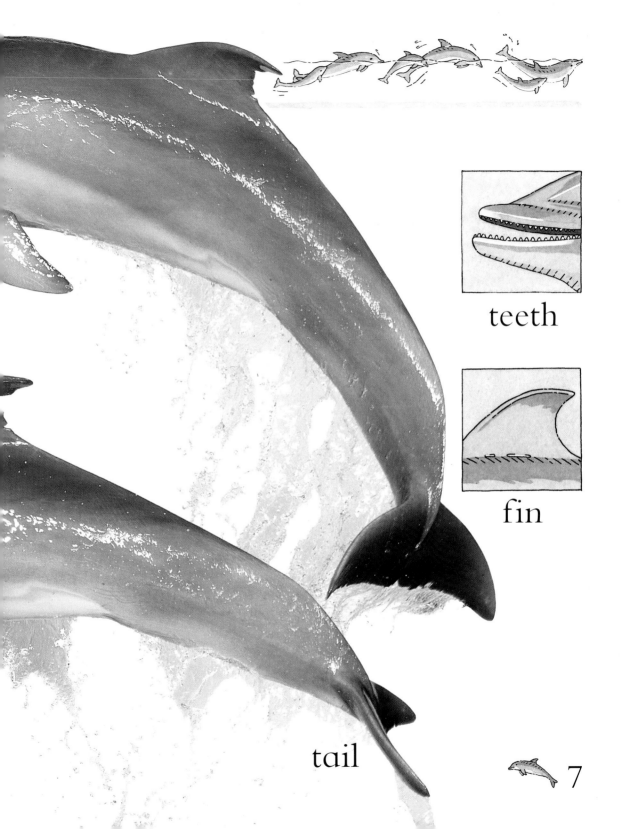

teeth

fin

tail

7

Crab

Crabs live at the ocean's edge. They hide in rock pools or burrow in the sand. Crabs have a hard shell that protects them. They move sideways, scampering along on their eight legs. A crab uses its pincers to catch shellfish and other food.

 8

shell

legs

pincer

9

Clownfish

Clownfish live near
coral reefs in warm seas.
They eat plankton and other
plants. Clownfish stay close
to the tentacles of an
animal called a sea
anemone. The sea anemone
stings the clownfish's enemies
in exchange for some of
the clownfish's food.

coral

scales

fin

 11

Seagull

Seagulls live in flocks at the seashore. They swoop and glide as they fly through the air. Seagulls will eat almost anything. Sometimes they steal their food from other birds. Seagulls lay their eggs in nests made of grass, twigs, and seaweed.

feathers

beak

leg

foot

13

Sea lion

Sea lions spend time both in the sea and on land. Their sleek bodies and large front flippers make them fast swimmers. On land, sea lions move slowly, using all four flippers to help them flop along. Sea lions eat fish and squid.

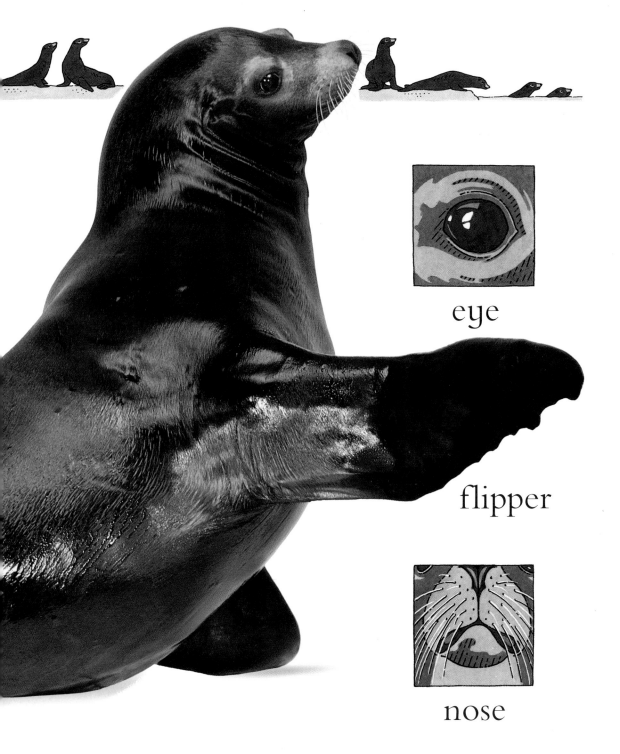

eye

flipper

nose

 15

Bullhead shark

This small bullhead shark has a big head and a flat nose. It eats shellfish, crabs, and other sea animals, grinding them up with its strong teeth. Sharks have a good sense of smell. This helps them to hunt for food.

fin

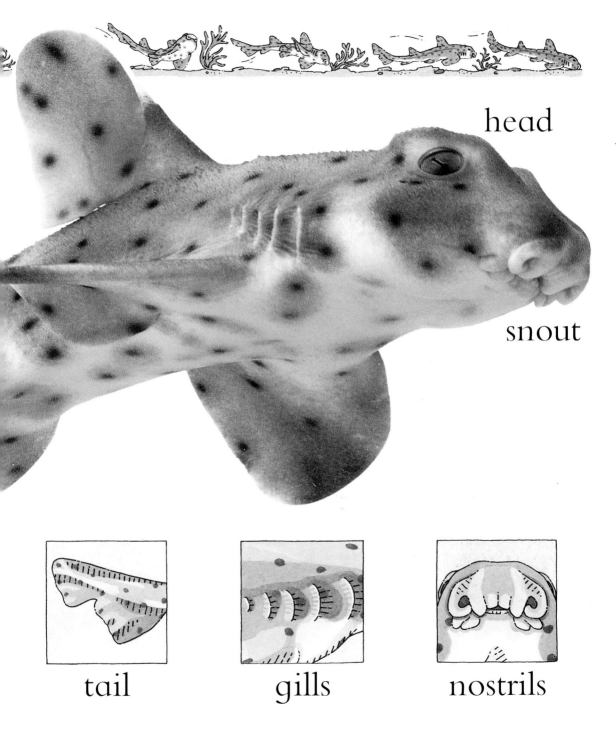

head

snout

tail

gills

nostrils

Starfish

Most starfish have five
arms. The underside of
each arm is covered
in suckers. The
starfish uses its
suckers to move
along the seabed and to pull
apart shellfish. The starfish
feeds itself through its mouth
in the middle of its underside.

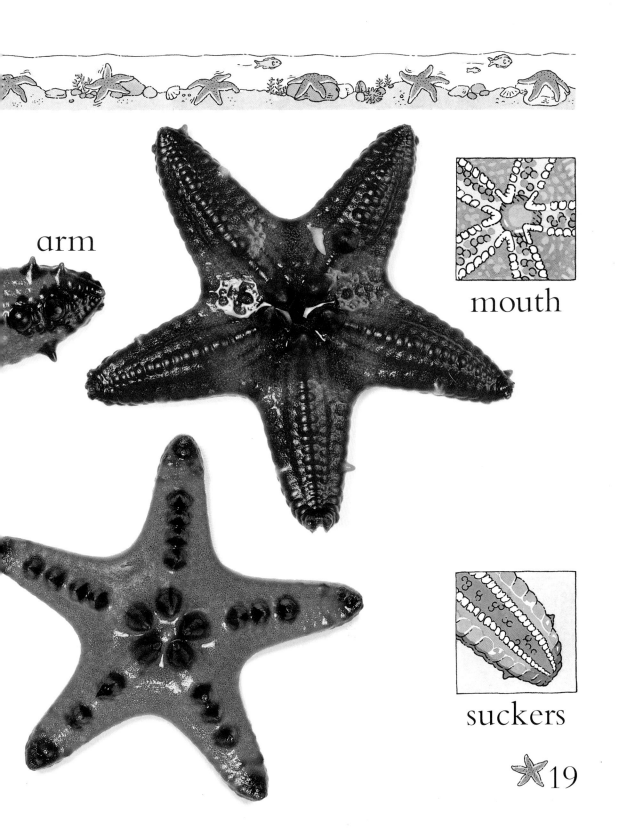

arm

mouth

suckers

*19

Sea horse

These fish are called sea horses because of the shape of their heads. They suck food up into their tube-shaped mouths. Sea horses swim upright, drifting in the sea. When they rest, sea horses coil their tails around sea plants.

head

spines

20

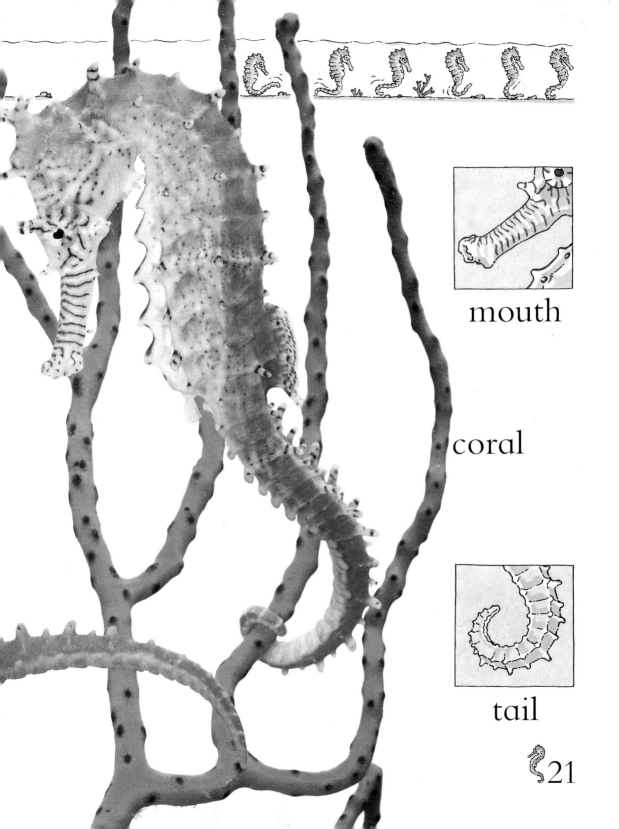

mouth

coral

tail

21